CUMBRIA LIBRARIES
3 8003 047

Magic
Animal Friends

For Haley and Anna Graves

Special thanks to Valerie Wilding

ORCHARD BOOKS

First published in Great Britain in 2016 by The Watts Publishing Group

1 3 5 7 9 10 8 6 4 2

Text copyright © Working Partners Ltd 2016
Illustrations copyright © Working Partners Ltd 2016
Series created by Working Partners Ltd

The moral rights of the author and illustrator have been asserted.
All characters and events in this publication, other than those clearly in the public domain, are fictitious and any resemblance to real persons, living or dead, is purely coincidental.

All rights reserved.
No part of this publication may be reproduced, stored in a retrieval system, or transmitted, in any form or by any means, without the prior permission in writing of the publisher, nor be otherwise circulated in any form of binding or cover other than that in which it is published and without a similar condition including this condition being imposed on the subsequent purchaser.

A CIP catalogue record for this book is available from the British Library.

ISBN 978 1 40834 117 9

Printed in Great Britain

The paper and board used in this book are made from wood from responsible sources

Orchard Books
An imprint of Hachette Children's Group
Part of The Watts Publishing Group Limited
Carmelite House, 50 Victoria Embankment, London EC4Y 0DZ

An Hachette UK Company
www.hachette.co.uk
www.hachettechildrens.co.uk

Phoebe Paddlefoot Makes a Splash

Daisy Meadows

To Friendship Forest
Shimmer Lake
Swimming School
Swimming
Beach
Pier

Map of Sapphire Isle
Bubbling Brook
Bucket and Spade Shop
Prettywhiskers' Purrfect Ice Cream Parlour
Shimmer Lake
Admiral Greatwing's House
To Grizelda's Tower

Can you keep a secret? I thought you could!

Then I'll tell you about an enchanted wood.

It lies through the door in the old oak tree,

Let's go there now - just follow me!

We'll find adventure that never ends,

And meet the Magic Animal Friends!

Love,

Goldie the Cat

Contents

CHAPTER ONE

Return to Sapphire Isle

The autumn sun was warm on Lily Hart's back as she fished a smooth, honey-coloured stone from Brightley Stream. She passed it to her best friend, Jess Forester, who put it in a basket.

"We've got loads of stones now," said

Jess with a happy smile.

"Yes, we'll need another basket soon!" said Lily.

The stream was at the bottom of the Harts' garden, behind the Helping Paw Wildlife Hospital. Lily's parents ran the hospital in their big barn, and both girls loved to help care for all the poorly animals. They had helped their parents build a new pond there for the ducklings and goslings to enjoy as they got better. They hoped it would have plenty of visiting creatures, too – newts, frogs, toads, and even swans!

Jess stood on one of the stepping stones that crossed the stream. She peered into the crystal-clear water at grey stones with orange threads running through them. "Look at these," she said. "They'd make such a pretty border around the pond."

Lily jumped onto the stepping stone beside Jess to look. Then something jumped onto Lily's stepping stone!

It was a beautiful cat with a golden coat and eyes the colour of fresh grass.

"Goldie!" Lily cried in delight.

The cat curled around her legs. Then she did the same to Jess, before leaping to the far bank and into Brightley Meadow.

"She's come to take us to Friendship Forest!" cried Jess.

The forest was their special secret – a magical world where animals lived in little cottages and sipped blackberry tea in the Toadstool Café. And, best of all, they could talk!

Lily and Jess raced after Goldie towards

a bare, lifeless tree in the middle of the meadow. The Friendship Tree!

As Goldie reached the tree, crisp yellow and crimson leaves sprang from the branches. A flock of squabbling jackdaws swooped down to feast on the berries that appeared, and pink autumn crocuses dotted the grass below.

The girls held hands and read two words written into the tree's bark.

"Friend...ship... Fore...est!" they said.

A door appeared in the trunk. Lily's eyes sparkled as she reached for the leaf-shaped handle and turned it.

Golden light shone out.

The cat leapt through the doorway, and the girls followed into the shimmering glow. They tingled all over, and squeezed each other's hands in excitement, knowing that the tingle meant they were shrinking a little.

As the light faded they found themselves in a woodland glade, surrounded by trees and brightly coloured flowers. The air was warm and sweetly scented.

And there was Goldie, standing upright and wearing her glittery scarf!

"Hello, Jess and Lily," she said in her soft voice. "Welcome back to Friendship Forest!"

The girls hugged her.

"It's so lovely to be with you again!" cried Jess.

"I hope Grizelda's not been causing trouble," said Lily.

Grizelda was an evil witch who wanted to get rid of the animals and take Friendship Forest for herself. So far Goldie and the girls had managed to stop her, but she never seemed to give up. On their last visit to the forest, Grizelda had stolen a magic sapphire that protected beautiful Sapphire Isle. It kept the water of Shimmer Lake at the perfect temperature. When Grizelda stole it, the lake had frozen and the beach had iced over, but luckily the girls and Goldie had managed to get the sapphire back.

"Are the other three sapphires safe?

Grizelda's bound to be after them, for sure," said Jess.

"Don't worry," said Goldie. "I asked the three families who look after them to be sure to hide them well."

"That's good," said Lily. But then she frowned, confused. "So why have you brought us here today?"

Goldie smiled. "Because we're joining the Sapphire Isle Boat Parade! Come on!"

The girls eagerly followed their friend through the forest.

"A boat parade sounds fun!" said Jess. "What happens?"

"The animals all sail around the island in boats they've made themselves," said Goldie.

"Wow!" said both girls at once.

They emerged from the forest to find a crystal-clear lake with a lush green island in the centre – Sapphire Isle. At the edge of the lake bobbed a pretty blue and yellow barge. A family of ducks waved from the deck.

"It's the Featherbills!" said Jess.

Little Ellie Featherbill hopped up and down, quacking. She was so excited she almost jumped out of her tiny red wellies. "Hello, Jess and Lily!" she called. "We're taking you and Goldie across the lake. Are you ready?"

"Yes!" the girls cried. "Thank you!"

Jess and Lily climbed on deck amid a flurry of feathery hugs from Ellie and her seven duckling brothers and sisters.

"Look at all the boats!" Ellie cried, pointing with a wingtip.

Boats of all different shapes and

sizes floated on the lake's waters. The Nibblesqueak hamsters waved from a little sailing boat, decorated with shiny nutshells. The Scruffypup family rowed like mad, trying to catch up with the Muddlepup family's paddleboat.

As they drew closer to the island, they waved to Mr Cleverfeather the owl, who wore a lifejacket over his waistcoat. His boat was shaped like a huge nest. A horn

on the front hooted when he squeezed it, and three chimneys each puffed out different coloured smoke.

Jess giggled. "He must have brought along some of his inventions."

"He's also brought Admiral Greatwing," said Lily, pointing to an elderly albatross. "Hello, Admiral!" she called.

"Ahoy there, shipmates!" he replied, in his booming voice.

"Date grey for boating!" called Mr Cleverfeather.

"He means, 'Great day for boating!'" giggled Jess.

As they reached the island's jetty, the girls found lots more animals watching the boats arrive.

Jess sighed happily as they stepped ashore. "It's going to be a lovely day."

Lily nodded. "And there's no sign of Grizelda to spoil it!"

CHAPTER TWO

Phoebe's Sapphire Secret

"Someone's waiting for us," said Goldie, pointing to a sailboat made of polished planks of yellow wood. Mounted in the middle of the deck was a steering wheel on a big wooden stand. On the pointed front of the boat was a wooden seahorse.

A smiling beaver wearing a red and blue striped jacket and matching cap waved from the deck. "Welcome aboard!" he called.

Goldie led the girls up the gangplank, and the beaver held out a paw to help them.

"Hello!" he said. "I'm Mr Paddlefoot, and I've heard all about you from my brother. He's one of the river Paddlefoots!" He looked over the side. "Now where's—"

Whoosh!

A small furry brown creature shot out of the water and landed on deck. She had

bright eyes, a tiny brown nose and little round ears. She shook herself, spraying water over everybody, then laughed a little tinkly laugh.

"Sorry!" she said. "I was visiting my friends at the bottom of the lake."

Goldie smiled as she flicked water droplets from her whiskers. "This is Phoebe Paddlefoot," she said. "Phoebe, meet Jess and Lily."

The little beaver threw her arms around the girls, who hugged her back.

"Oops!" she said. "I forgot I was wet!

"That's OK, we're—" Lily tried to say, but Phoebe was still speaking.

"My cousins Betsy and Bobby told me how they helped you save Molly Twinkletail the mouse from the boggits," Phoebe said excitedly. "I'd love to have a whizzo-fizzo adventure with you too!" Hardly pausing for breath, she added, "Dad and I built our boat. Do you like it?"

"It's beautiful!" Jess and Lily said

together, sharing a smile. Phoebe could talk very fast!

"Come on!" called Phoebe. "Let me show you around!" She pulled them this way and that around the boat. "Here's our cupboard, and our ropes, and our picnic box – yum yum – and our tool chest ..." Finally, she whispered, "There's another thing, but it's secret. This way."

The girls and Goldie followed Phoebe to the steering wheel stand. Phoebe tapped on it three times, and a hidden compartment sprang open.

Boing!

The girls jumped in surprise. "Wow!" said Jess.

In the compartment was a beautiful blue shell. Phoebe opened it to reveal a brilliant blue gem, shaped like a droplet of water. It flashed and glittered in the sunlight.

"Is that one of the magical sapphires

that guard the island?" asked Lily.

Phoebe nodded. "Dad and I guard this sapphire. It keeps the lake clean and crystal clear. If anything happened to it the lake would turn to horrid muck, and all of the animals who live on the lake bottom would have to leave."

"It's a very important job, Phoebe," said Jess seriously.

The little beaver nodded. "We know Grizelda stole the Prettywhiskers' sapphire, so we're being extra sure to keep our one hidden." Then she grinned. "Dad and I have another important task, too," she said. "We're expert boat-builders, so we judge the boat parade. The first prize is a golden flag which flies on the winning boat for a whole year! Ooh!" She put her paws to her mouth. "Would you three like to help with the judging?"

Jess, Lily and Goldie glanced at each other, thrilled. "We'd love to!"

"Great!" Phoebe put the sapphire back in its shell and shut it in its compartment.

Suddenly, they heard a raspy horn blow. The girls, Goldie and Phoebe stared out across the lake, following the noise, and saw a steamboat approaching.

"But all the animals who have entered the parade are here already," said Phoebe. "Who could that be? And who would enter such a horrible boat in the parade?"

The boat was covered with slimy seaweed and its flag had a cauldron and two crossed brooms. Its funnel gave another blast that sounded like a hundred rusty trumpets, then spurted yellow sparks.

The girls looked at each other in

dismay. They knew who it was.

"Grizelda!" groaned Lily.

The witch stood at the front of the boat, steering it towards Sapphire Isle. Her green hair blew behind her, and her black cloak swirled over her purple top and skinny black trousers.

The animals on the shore and in the other boats

all started crying out in fear.

"The witch is here!"

"What does she want?"

"She'll ruin our parade!"

Lily and Jess recognised the four tiny water imps who stood beside the witch, laughing. They had blue skin, and wore tattered trousers, stripy tops and hats. They each carried a bucket with something green and slimy slopping over the top.

"Argh!" cried Kelp, the first imp, waving his seaweed net.

"Heave, ho!" screeched Urchin,

tightening her belt of water bombs.

"Thar she blows!" yelled Barnacle, pointing at Phoebe's boat.

"And shiver me timbers!" added

Shrimp, the smallest imp. He was wearing yellow armbands.

Jess and Lily exchanged a worried

look. They knew Grizelda's imps loved treasure.

"I hope they aren't coming for Phoebe's sapphire!" whispered Lily.

The boat stopped, and Grizelda threw back her head, cackling with laughter. "Ha ha! It's the meddling girls and their interfering cat. Kelp, you and the rest of the imps get to the cannons."

Kelp led the imps across the deck, stomping on his wooden leg. He pulled a cloth aside, revealing a large cannon. Urchin did the same. Barnacle used her sticky hands to somersault over to her cannon, and little Shrimp waddled over to another.

Lily and Jess were horrified. Grizelda was going to fire at the boats!

"Give me the sapphires!" Grizelda yelled, stamping her feet.

"Not a chance!" Jess yelled back.

"If you don't, I'll sink all the boats, one after the other," Grizelda said, smiling smugly. "And I won't stop until you tell me where I can find a sapphire!"

Kelp, Urchin, Barnacle and Shrimp howled with laughter.

Grizelda turned to the imps. "Seaweed bombs ready?"

Four cannons swivelled and took aim straight at the Paddlefoots' boat!

CHAPTER THREE

Shipwreck!

The girls, Goldie and the Paddlefoots stared in horror.

"Quickly, Phoebe!" cried Mr Paddlefoot. "Get to the compartment!"

Phoebe dashed toward the secret cubby beneath the steering wheel but, before she could reach it, Grizelda cackled.

"Silly beavers," she sneered. "What's so important you have to hide it in a secret compartment, eh? It's the sapphire!"

She turned to the imps. "Fire!"

Boosh! Boosh! Boosh! Boosh!

The four cannons blasted away. They shot bombs of smelly seaweed and fierce jets of filthy water.

Lily and Jess dived onto the deck to take cover.

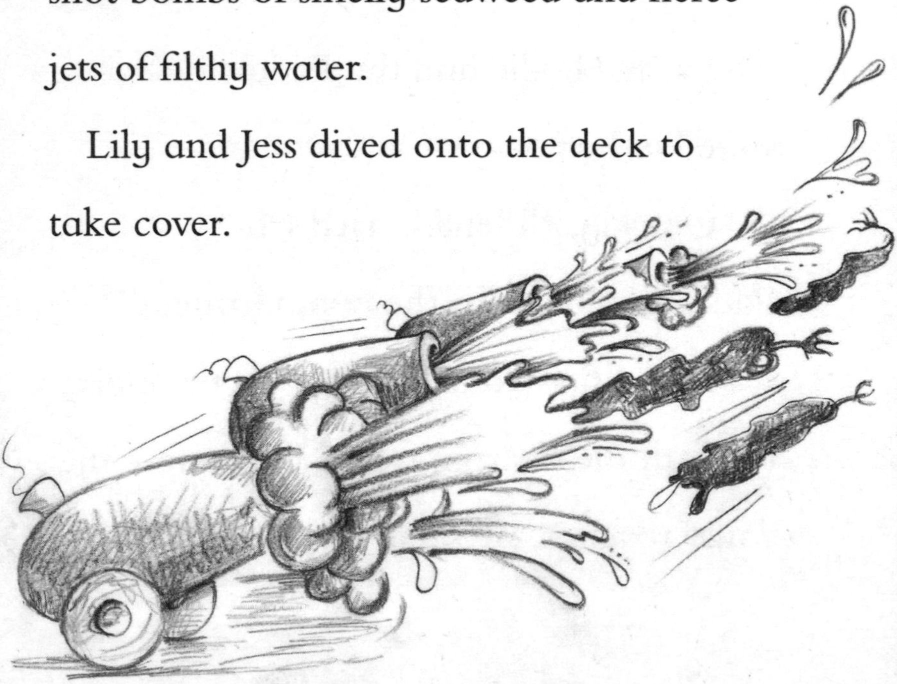

"Please stop them!" Phoebe shouted. "They'll sink us!"

More seaweed bombs hit their target and more dirty water swamped the deck. The boat rocked dangerously.

Mr Paddlefoot staggered across the deck. "Hold on!" he shouted. "We don't want anyone washed overboard."

He grasped Phoebe with one paw and the boat rail with the other. The girls and Goldie gripped the mast as the boat lurched from side to side.

Grizelda's steamboat came closer.

Boosh! Boosh! Boosh! Boosh!

The Paddlefoots' boat rocked even more wildly.

Phoebe screamed, "The bombs have made holes in our boat!"

"It'll sink!" shrieked Grizelda. "And take the sapphire with it!"

The mean witch sailed right up to the Paddlefoots' boat. The imps leapt aboard.

"Stop right there, you horrible imps!" Jess yelled. She tried to grab one of them but the boat was tilting upright. They were sinking fast.

Hoot! Hoot!

The friends spun around to see Mr Cleverfeather's boat alongside them.

"Come aboard!" boomed Admiral Greatwing from the deck, reaching out to Phoebe.

But she pulled away. "There's something I've got to do!" she cried, and stumbled towards the secret compartment.

"She's trying to save the sapphire!" cried Lily.

"Quickly, Phoebe! Before the boat goes under!" Jess yelled, as Phoebe tapped on the compartment.

Boing!

It sprang open and the blue shell slid out. It hit the tilting deck and opened up. The droplet-shaped sapphire fell out and bounced along the deck.

"Catch it!" cried Lily.

Phoebe lunged towards it. But the boat tilted again, and she snatched at the steering wheel to save herself.

"We've got to get off the boat!" yelled Mr Paddlefoot. "There's no more time!"

He grabbed Phoebe's paw. Goldie, Jess and Lily joined paws and hands into a chain, and Lily held onto Mr Paddlefoot. With Admiral Greatwing's help, they all managed to climb aboard Mr Cleverfeather's boat.

Jess and Lily looked back in dismay. The Paddlefoots' boat was sinking, and

the sapphire was going with it!

The four imps stood to attention on the deck. As the boat vanished beneath the lake's surface, they disappeared too.

"Ha haa!" Grizelda cackled. "My imps will get that sapphire! They'll take it where you'll never find it!"

The crystal-clear water was already turning sludgy brown.

"The animals won't want to live by the lake any more," Grizelda shrieked. "So they'll leave the island. Then I'll build my holiday home – Sorcery Tower! Ha haa!"

She screeched with laughter and spun her steering wheel. The slimy boat sailed across the lake, which was now covered with a scum of rotting weeds.

Mr Paddlefoot, Captain Greatwing, Goldie and Mr Cleverfeather stared after it, shaking their heads in dismay.

The girls went over and hugged Phoebe, who was in tears.

"Our boat's sunk," the little beaver sobbed, "and – and …" She struggled to speak. "Grizelda's imps have got the sapphire!"

Jess wiped Phoebe's cheeks. "Don't worry," she said kindly. "We won't let Grizelda get away with her horrible plan."

"We'll find your sapphire," Lily promised. "And I've an idea how!"

Everyone stared. "How?" they asked together.

"Do you remember Admiral Greatwing's magical map?" said Lily. "It

shows where the sapphires are. We can use that to see where the imps have taken it, can't we, Admiral?"

The albatross shook his head. "By my feathers, I wish you could," he boomed. "But the map only shows the island and the lake's surface. While the sapphire is underwater, it's useless."

"So wow not?" asked Mr Cleverfeather. "I mean, now what?"

"I don't know," said Goldie. "But unless we get the sapphire back, the lake will be ruined for ever!"

CHAPTER FOUR

Mr Cleverfeather's Brilliant Bubble Heads

Phoebe peered down at the murky water. "All my poor friends on the lake bottom!" she cried. "It's so dirty, they'll hardly be able to see anything."

"Maybe the dirt means the imps haven't spotted the sapphire yet," said Lily.

Jess nodded. "Let's swim down to Phoebe's boat and find it first!"

"But it's so deep," said Goldie doubtfully. "We'd never hold our breath for long enough."

"Hoo!" Mr Cleverfeather hooted. "I've the very thing! Hubble beds!" He flapped his wings. "I mean, bubble heads!"

Jess and Lily exchanged puzzled glances. "Bubble heads?"

The elderly owl lifted a seat and produced four bubble-shaped helmets from a compartment underneath. "These will let you stay underwater as long as

you want. You can even talk to each other through them. "

"Amazing!" said Lily, as she, Goldie and Jess took one. "Thanks, Mr Cleverfeather."

"Dad!" cried Phoebe. "I can go, can't I? The girls and Goldie will need someone to help them find their way underwater, and I know the bottom of the lake better than anyone because I've got lots of friends there." She looked serious. "If we don't find the sapphire, their homes will be ruined."

"All right," said Mr Paddlefoot. "Mr Cleverfeather and I will wait here with

Admiral Greatwing in case Grizelda returns."

Jess and Lily helped Phoebe and Goldie put on their bubble heads, then put their own on.

"This feels very strange," said Jess. "Can everyone hear me?"

"Yes!" answered the others.

They held hands and paws, and after a "One, two, three..." from Goldie, they jumped overboard.

Swirls of muck clouded the water.

"I can usually see to the bottom," said Phoebe, "but it's too dirty to see anything much now."

"Let's hold on to each other, so we don't get separated," said Jess. "Phoebe, you lead the way."

The little beaver swam downwards, and soon the girls found

themselves at the bottom of the lake.

The lake bed was covered in plants that looked brown in the muck.

"It's even gloomier down here," said Jess. "Can anyone see anything?"

"Yes!" said Lily, pointing to a shadowy shape. "Is that the Paddlefoots' boat?"

"Let's go and see," said Phoebe.

They followed her towards the eerie shadow. When they had almost reached it, the little beaver cried, "It *is* our boat!"

"Careful, everyone," Goldie warned. "The imps might be near. If they've found the sapphire, we'll need to follow them.

They mustn't see us."

They swam cautiously towards the wreck, listening for any sign of the imps. But the lake was strangely quiet.

They swam inside the hull of the boat and looked around. The mast had fallen over, blocking their way.

"There!" cried Jess. "Behind the mast – I can see the blue shell. Maybe the sapphire's nearby!"

Lily groaned. "But we can't reach it. Not even Phoebe's little enough."

"Then how can we get it?" asked Jess, batting away a clump of seaweed that dangled in front of her bubble head.

Phoebe thought for a moment. "I've got a whizzo-fizzo idea!" she said. "I'll chew through the mast. Then you can pull it aside!"

"Great idea, Phoebe!" cried Lily.

Phoebe took a deep breath and removed her helmet. She handed it to Lily with a thumbs up,

and set to work.

The girls watched, amazed, as Phoebe chewed and gnawed and scraped at the wood with her strong front teeth. In next to no time, the mast was in two jagged pieces, and Phoebe waved her hand at Lily to signal for her helmet back. She breathed deeply once it was back on.

Goldie pulled out the blue shell. She opened it but it was empty. Then she felt around where the shell had been. When she looked back at the girls, her whiskers had drooped.

"The sapphire's not there," she said.

Jess put her arm around Phoebe. "At least we have the shell. We'll need it to make the sapphire's magic work."

Phoebe nodded. "I'll take the shell up to Mr Cleverfeather's boat," she said. "Dad will keep it safe."

With a flick of her tail, she disappeared up into the murk. The girls and Goldie thought hard about where to search for the sapphire next – and they were still thinking when Phoebe came swimming back towards them.

"Dad's pleased about the shell," she said, "but what about the sapphire? Will

we ever find it?"

Lily cuddled her, their two bubble heads close together. "It's down here somewhere," she said. "And we aren't leaving until we find it!"

Goldie gave a cry. "Look, up ahead! Specks of light! See?"

Jess peered through the gloom. "It must be the imps."

"Of course!" said Lily. "Who else would be swimming around in this murky water?"

"They must have taken the sapphire!" Jess cried. "Come on! After them!"

CHAPTER FIVE

Mrs Greenshell's School of Fish

Phoebe, Goldie and the girls swam towards the lights. As they drew near, Jess said, "Let's stop and listen. Maybe we'll hear what the imps have done with the sapphire."

But instead of Kelp and Barnacle's

noisy squabbling, or Shrimp and Urchin singing sea shanties, they heard lots of tiny, scared voices.

Then a stronger voice said, "Don't be afraid, little ones! Stay in pairs and follow me!"

Phoebe gasped. "That's Mrs Greenshell the teacher, with her School of Fish! The lights must be coming from the glowfish in her class."

"Maybe they saw where the imps went!" Lily said hopefully. "Let's ask."

Phoebe led them towards the lights. They were met by a large turtle, wearing

an enormous pair of glasses studded with tiny shells.

"Hello, Mrs Greenshell," said Phoebe.

The turtle removed her glasses and wiped slimy muck from them. "Phoebe, dear," she said. "Is that you? The lake's in such a terrible state, I can barely see you." She clapped her fins. "Class! Say hello to Phoebe and her friends."

"Hello, Phoebe and her friends!" the class chanted.

There were shining glowfish and tiny pink, purple, red and green starfish, who were pulling strands of seaweed

off each other. Four yellow and orange octopuses blocked the muck by covering their mouths with their bright, squishy tentacles, and a group of guppies clustered together, grumbling about the dirty water. Four hermit crabs at the back of the class had retreated into their shells. Only their eyes could be seen, gleaming from inside.

"I didn't know sea creatures lived here, too," Jess whispered.

Goldie smiled. "They love the lake's magical waters!"

Mrs Greenshell wiped her glasses again. "Keep together, class," she said. "I can

hardly see you."

"We're sorry about all the muck," said Lily. Then she explained how Grizelda's water imps had stolen the sapphire.

"If those imps were in my class," said Mrs Greenshell, "I would teach them not to steal!"

"Did any of you see where the imps went?" asked Jess.

Mrs Greenshell turned to her class.

"Fins, arms or tentacles up if you've seen any water imps!"

The girls squinted through the dirty water, but no one moved.

"I'm sorry," said Mrs Greenshell. "We've been visiting the coral reef, and the lake's so dirty we're having trouble finding our way back to the schoolhouse. I'm worried I might lose someone."

She pushed a clump of muck aside and clapped her fins again. "Stay still, class, while I count you. Two... four... six... eight... ten... twelve..."

When Mrs Greenshell had finished, she

put a fin to her forehead, looking puzzled. "That's strange. I have four extra pupils!"

Jess and Lily heard wild giggling from the back of the class.

"Who's that?" demanded Mrs Greenshell.

"The hermit crabs?" Jess wondered aloud.

"No, it ain't!" shouted Kelp's voice. "It be us!"

Four shells were tossed aside, revealing four water imps clutching handfuls of seaweed! Their little blue faces creased with laughter as they shot towards the girls. In moments, they'd wrapped Phoebe, Jess, Lily and Goldie in long stringy weed.

"Har!" laughed Barnacle. "You be all of a tangle!"

"You think you be clever finding us," said Urchin, "but you won't catch us!"

And the imps zoomed off into the murk.

CHAPTER SIX

A Pirate Song

"I've never seen such behaviour in my life!" said Mrs Greenshell. She and her class rushed to help untangle the girls, Goldie and Phoebe from the seaweed.

"Thanks!" said Jess, as an octopus pulled the last strand from her ankle.

But. immediately, more clouds of muck

and stringy seaweed swirled around them all.

"The lake's getting dirtier," groaned Lily. "We'll never find the imps in this."

"Hey!" cried Phoebe. "I've got another whizzo-fizzo idea. Watch this!"

She swam around Mrs Greenshell's class using her wide, flat tail to swish away the weed.

"See?" she said. "I'll clear the muck, then the glowfish can swim behind me

and light the way for everyone else."

"That's a great idea!" said Lily. "And after we find the imps, we'll help everyone get back to the schoolhouse!"

"Wonderful!" said Mrs Greenshell. "Thank you."

Phoebe led the way, swishing her tail back and forth. The glowfish and the rest of the school followed, then Goldie, Jess and Lily.

Phoebe stopped suddenly. The fish,

octopuses and starfish bumped into her, then Mrs Greenshell, Goldie and the girls bumped into them.

"Ow!" cried an octopus.

"Hey!" yelped a glowfish.

"What's going on?" asked a starfish.

Jess, Lily, and Goldie swam ahead to see Phoebe talking to an elderly seahorse in a green apron. He carried a garden rake and was frowning crossly.

"This is Mr Spinytail, the gardener," explained Phoebe.

"What's wrong?" asked Lily.

Mr Spinytail pointed to a bed of

beautifully coloured anemones: palest pink, butter yellow, midnight blue and deep purple. Many lay on their sides, their tentacles drooping. The lake bed underneath them had been churned up.

Mr Spinytail frowned. "Some horrible little imps found it funny to zoom around my garden. Disgraceful behaviour! It's hard enough for my poor anemones to survive in this mucky water, without those horrible imps behaving like hooligans!"

"Quite right!" said Mrs Greenshell. "If this filth isn't cleared soon, none of us will be able to live down here."

Jess leaned down to help untangle two starfish who were stuck together. "We're doing everything we can to save the lake," she said. "At least we know we're heading in the right direction."

They thanked Mr Spinytail and left him tidying his anemones. Soon they reached the dark mouth of a cave.

Lily went to peer inside, but Goldie put

a paw on her arm. "Wait," she said. "Listen. Someone's in there."

The girls tipped their bubble heads towards the cave and listened.

From inside, they heard:

"Four little pirates, oh so clever,

Sailing the seas forever and ever.

One found some gold and laughed with glee,

He bought himself an island, and then there were three.

Hoy!

Three little pirates, oh so clever,

Looking for treasure forever and ever.

One found some jewels and cried,

'That'll do!'

He bought himself a big ship and then there were two.

Hoy!"

"It's the imps!" whispered Lily. "Maybe they'll mention the sapphire."

As the song finished, Urchin give a great cackle followed by a very loud burp. "Hee hee, us will soon have our ship. All we have to do is give Grizelda the sapphire."

"Best to be locking it away in our treasure chest, Urchin," came Barnacle's voice. "We be in big trouble if we loses it."

There was the sound of a heavy lid banging shut, then the clunk of a key turning.

"It be safe now," said Shrimp. "No one can get it."

Jess signalled to the others to join her behind a slime-covered rock.

"The imps are treasure-mad," she said. "They're so pleased with that sapphire, maybe they'd leave the cave if they thought there was another one nearby."

Lily's face brightened. "That could work!" she said. "And I think I know how!"

Mrs Greenshell gathered her class and joined Jess, Goldie and Phoebe to listen to the plan.

Lily began to whisper. "This is what we'll do …"

CHAPTER SEVEN

The Treasure Chest

Goldie, Phoebe and the girls bobbed in the water just above the cave entrance.

Jess took a deep breath. "It's too bad we couldn't find the sapphire the imps took," she said loudly.

"Yes," Lily said clearly. "But if we hadn't followed them, we'd never have spotted that other sapphire. It's much better!"

Goldie winked at the others. "It's so glittery and shiny!"

Phoebe grinned. "Yes, so much sparklier than the one those silly imps took!"

Jess looked down to see the imps hovering at the cave entrance. They were listening!

She gave the others a nod. They waited for the imps to creep close enough to see them clearly, and then Lily pointed to where the light of the glowfish sparkled through the dirty water a little way away.

"See how the sapphire's shining through the muck," she said loudly. "Quick! Let's get it before anyone else does!"

The girls held their breath. Then, just as they'd hoped, the imps zoomed out of the cave, swimming towards the light.

Jess giggled. "I wish I could see their faces when they realise they're chasing after glowfish!"

Once the imps were out of sight, Goldie, Phoebe and the girls swam into the cave. Right at the end, nestled among some pebbles, they saw a wooden chest with golden clasps. It was old and battered, with a big metal lock.

"The sapphire must be inside!" said Jess.

"But there's no key," said Lily. "How can we open it?"

"Phoebe can do it," said Goldie. "Just like with the ship's mast!"

Phoebe breathed in deeply, removed her bubble head and handed it to Jess. Then

she set to work with her strong front teeth, gnawing and chewing at the chest, then gnawing and chewing some more. But soon she gestured to Jess to hand her the bubble head.

"This wood's very strong!" she said. "I can't chew through it! Now what?"

Everyone thought for a moment.

"I know!" Jess cried. "Your tail! Can

you thump it against the chest lid?"

The little beaver nodded. "I'll try!"

She turned around, raised her tail and thwacked it against the chest, once, twice and three times.

Finally, the lid splintered. Jess and Lily pulled at it, and it broke away.

Inside, gleaming, was the sapphire!

"Hooray!" everyone cheered.

They swam out of the cave to find Mrs Greenshell waiting for them.

"My glowfish are leading the imps in a watery dance," she said.

Looking up, they could just make out a

bright light zigzagging this way and that.

Lily showed the teacher the sapphire. "We've got to go back to the surface and put it in its shell," she said.

"I'll wait here," said Mrs Greenshell. "When the imps come back to the cave, I'll give them a scolding they'll never forget. I'll keep them in detention until the sapphire's safely in place."

The four friends thanked her for helping. "You'll know when we've done it," said Jess. "The water should start to clear."

"Then you'll be able to take your class

back to the schoolhouse," said Goldie.

"Perfect. We'll be back for break time," said Mrs Greenshell, nodding approvingly.

Phoebe, Goldie and the girls turned towards the surface.

"Keep together," Jess warned. "We mustn't get lost now."

"And, Lily, whatever happens," Goldie said with a grin, "don't drop that sapphire!"

CHAPTER EIGHT

Sapphire Surprise

Jess and Lily bobbed to the surface, then Phoebe and Goldie popped up, too.

Mr Paddlefoot, Admiral Greatwing and Mr Cleverfeather were leaning over the side of the owl's boat, looking for them.

"Ahoy there!" boomed Admiral Greatwing, as they all climbed aboard.

Lily reached into her pocket and pulled out the sapphire.

"By my feathers!" boomed Admiral Greatwing. "You got it back! Well done, shipmates!"

Mr Cleverfeather peered at the sapphire through his monocle. "I'm sad to glee that," he said, then hooted with laughter. "I mean, I'm glad to see that!"

Phoebe's dad held out the shell. "Let's put the sapphire where it belongs."

Lily passed the sapphire to Phoebe, and the little beaver carefully placed it inside.

Everyone held their breath as they

looked over at Shimmer Lake.

The rubbish on the top disappeared, weeds and leaves sank out of sight and the water grew cleaner. Soon it was crystal-clear and sparkling again.

"Hooray!" everyone cried.

Mr Paddlefoot looked proudly at his daughter. "You and you friends have saved the lake," he said.

"We couldn't have done it without Phoebe," said Lily.

"Yes," said Jess. "She's very talented!"

There were cries of, "The sapphire's back!" from the beach, and the girls

waved to all the animals gathered there.

But, suddenly, the cheers changed to gasps, and everyone stared across the lake.

The girls turned to see a slimy, seaweed-covered boat, spitting yellow sparks from its funnel.

"Grizelda!" cried Jess.

"Everyone keep back," Goldie said.

The witch steamed towards Mr Cleverfeather's boat, and shook her bony fists. "You might have stopped my imps," she screeched, "but I'll be back! Next time, no one will stop me!"

Jess drew herself up tall. "We will!" she

shouted bravely.

In reply, Grizelda's steamboat gave a rusty trumpet blast as it sailed away.

Goldie, the girls, the admiral, Mr Cleverfeather and Mr Paddlefoot joined hands and paws in a dance of delight.

But Phoebe sat sadly to one side.

"Aren't you happy the lake's clean again?" Lily asked gently.

"Yes," said Phoebe. "But our boat's wrecked, and I'll miss sailing with Dad."

Mr Cleverfeather laughed. "Book at the leach, Phoebe. I mean, look at the beach!"

Everyone else looked, too. There, by the shore, was a shimmering silver sail boat.

"It's beautiful!" said Jess.

Admiral Greatwing folded his wings over his chest. "That boat, shipmates," he said, "is Phoebe's boat!"

The little beaver gasped. "Mine?"

Her dad hugged her. "It's made of different pieces of everybody else's boats."

The girls recognised parts from all the boats they'd seen before – blue planks from the Featherbills' barge, a waterlily leaf sail from the Greenhop frogs, and oars from the Prettywhiskers. It seemed as though every animal in Friendship Forest had contributed something.

"But who built it?" asked Jess.

"Me!" said Mr Cleverfeather. "I used my Cobbler Contraption. It cobbled it together in toe nime. I mean, no time."

Phoebe clapped her paws. "It's the best boat ever!"

The girls, Goldie and the Paddlefoots

went ashore, and all the animals crowded around, thanking them for their help.

Admiral Greatwing flew onto a big rock. "But wait, everyone!" he boomed. "We have one more surprise!"

The animals fell quiet. They were all smiling and staring at the Paddlefoots.

"The animals have voted, and we have agreed that the winners of this year's Boat Parade should be – the Paddlefoots!"

Jess and Lily hugged Phoebe.

"Well done!" cried Jess.

"You deserve it," said Lily, giving Phoebe a hug.

The Scruffypup family carried the little beaver shoulder-high as cheers rang out.

Phoebe cried, "Three cheers for Goldie and the girls. We'd never have got the sapphire back without them!"

Then Mrs Prettywhiskers called, "Ice creams for everybody at Prettywhiskers Purrfect Ice Cream Parlour!"

Jess and Lily enjoyed cones of their favourite ice cream: mint chocolate chip for Lily and cherry for Jess. Goldie had her favourite, too – strawberry hazelnut.

Afterwards, Mr Paddlefoot invited Goldie and the girls to join him and Phoebe on the new boat. They said goodbye to Mr Cleverfeather and Admiral Greatwing and jumped aboard.

"We're calling our boat *Sapphire Surprise*," said Phoebe. She giggled. "That's because we'd be surprised if anyone finds the sapphire now!"

Lily and Jess looked around. There

didn't seem to be anywhere to hide it.

"Where is the sapphire?" asked Goldie.

Mr Paddlefoot slowly lifted his cap. There, nestling on top of his furry head, was the brilliant blue shell. He grinned. "The sapphire's safely inside!"

Everyone laughed as Phoebe sailed the new boat back to Friendship Forest. The sparkling blue lake was calm and clear. When they arrived on shore, Phoebe held out two handfuls of pretty seashells

to the girls. "These are for you," she said. "I got them from the lake bottom when you were talking to Mrs Greenshell."

"They're lovely!" said Jess, hugging her. "Goodbye. Goodbye, Mr Paddlefoot."

Lily hugged the little beaver, too. "We'll come back soon," she promised.

The girls waved as *Sapphire Surprise* turned and sailed away. Then they followed Goldie back through the forest.

At the Friendship Tree, Goldie said, "Thank you for helping save Shimmer Lake and Sapphire Isle!"

Jess put her arms around the cat. "Just

fetch us if Grizelda tries any more tricks."

"She'd probably like to get her hands on the last two sapphires," said Lily. "But we'll be ready for her."

"I know you will," said Goldie. She hugged Lily. "See you soon!"

She touched the tree, and a door appeared in the trunk.

Jess opened it, letting golden light shine out. Thc girls stepped into the shimmering glow. Instantly, they felt the tingle that told them they were returning to their proper size.

The light faded and they stepped out

into Brightley Meadow.

Lily held Jess's hand and they ran back across the stream to Helping Paw. "We've got the perfect things to decorate the new pond with," she said.

"The seashells!" said Jess. "Of course! They'll make it the loveliest pond ever!"

The girls both knew that every time they saw the shells, they'd think of their amazing adventure with little Phoebe Paddlefoot.

The End

The waters of Shimmer Lake have turned wild and dangerous! Can tiny piglet Millie Picklesnout help Lily and Jess make it safe again for everyone in time for the Friendship Forest Funfair?

Find out in the next adventure,

Millie Picklesnout's Wild Ride

Turn over for a sneak peek . . .

"Let's fill it up!" said Lily Hart. She aimed the hose towards the big hole that was going to be a new pond.

Lily and her best friend, Jess Forester, were in the Harts' garden. Nearby was the Helping Paw Wildlife Hospital, which Lily's parents ran in a barn behind their cottage. The new pond was for the poorly ducklings who were staying there. The girls were sure that other creatures would use it, too – goslings, frogs, dragonflies and newts. All were welcome!

Lily held the hose ready as Jess crunched through crisp autumn leaves to turn on the garden tap. Water spurted out of the end of the hose and started to fill the pond.

"Quack! Quack! Quack!"

Three fluffy yellow ducklings waddled towards the pond. Lily wiggled the hose, splashing them a little. They quacked and flapped, enjoying their shower in the warm sunshine!

"Our first visitors!" said Jess with a laugh, as she hurried back to Lily.

Lily lay down the hose so it dangled over the pond's edge. "It'll take ages to fill," she said. "Why don't we—Listen!

Did you hear that?"

A soft mew came from behind them. The girls spun around to see a beautiful green-eyed cat. Her golden fur gleamed in the sunshine.

"Goldie!" cried Jess. "It's wonderful to see you again!"

Goldie was their special friend. She came from Friendship Forest – a secret, magical world where all the animals could talk! They lived in cosy dens and cottages, and loved chatting over honey milkshakes in the Toadstool Café. Goldie often took Jess and Lily there to visit their animal friends, and they'd shared many adventures.

The girls stroked the purring cat.

"She's come to take us to Friendship Forest!" said Lily, her eyes shining.

Jess grinned, but then she looked serious. "I just hope Grizelda isn't up to her old tricks," she said.

Read

Millie Picklesnout's Wild Ride

to find out what happens next!

Can Jess and Lily save the beautiful Sapphire Isle and Shimmer Lake from Grizelda? Read all of series five to find out!

COMING SOON!
Look out for
Jess and Lily's
next adventure:
Holly Santapaws Saves
Christmas!

www.magicanimalfriends.com

Jess and Lily's Animal Facts

Lily and Jess love lots of different animals – both in Friendship Forest and in the real world.

Here are their top facts about

BEAVERS

like Phoebe Paddlefoot:

- Beavers build dams from mud, stones and sticks to protect their homes from predators.
- Beavers have very strong front teeth, which never stop growing!
- Beavers are herbivores. They mostly eat twigs, tree bark and plants that grow in the water.
- A group of beavers is called a 'family'.

Magic Animal Friends

Can you keep the secret?

There's lots of fun for everyone at
www.magicanimalfriends.com

Play games and explore the secret world of Friendship Forest, where animals can talk!

Join the
Magic Animal Friends Club!

Special competitions

Exclusive content

All the latest Magic Animal Friends news!

To join the Club, simply go to

www.magicanimalfriends.com/join-our-club/

Terms and Conditions
(1) Open to UK and Republic of Ireland residents only (2) Please get the email of your parent/guardian to enter
(3) We may use your data to contact you with further offers

Full terms and conditions at www.hachettechildrensdigital.co.uk/terms/